AWESOME JOKES

FOR 9 YEAR OLDS

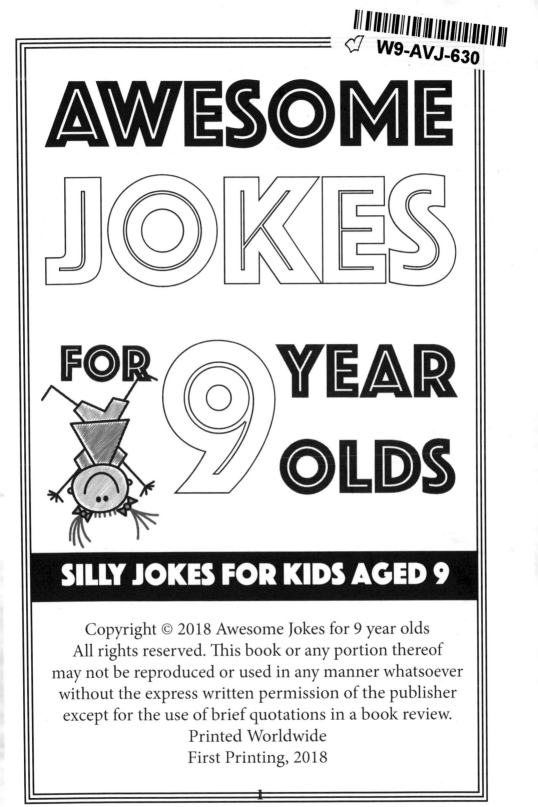

SILLY JOKES FOR KIDS AGED 9

What do you call a woman who catches butterflies?

a. Anette.

What did the psychology book say to the math book?

a. You've got problems.

Knock knock.
a. Who's there?
b. Goliath.
c. Goliath who?
d. Goliath down if you're tired.

Knock knock.
a. Who's there?
b. Lettuce.
c. Lettuce who?
d. Lettuce in please!

Knock knock.
a. Who's there?
b. Alpaca.
c. Alpaca who?
d. Alpaca bag, I'm leaving tomorrow.

What did 0 say when he saw 8?

a. I like your belt!

What do you call a pig that becomes a lumberjack?

a. Pork chop!

What is black and white and red all over?

a. A newspaper.

Mom: This onion is making me cry.

a. Kid: What did it say to you?

What did the snail say while it rode the tortoise?

a. "Weeeeeeeeeeeee!"

Why did the groom cross the road?

a. To get to the other bride.

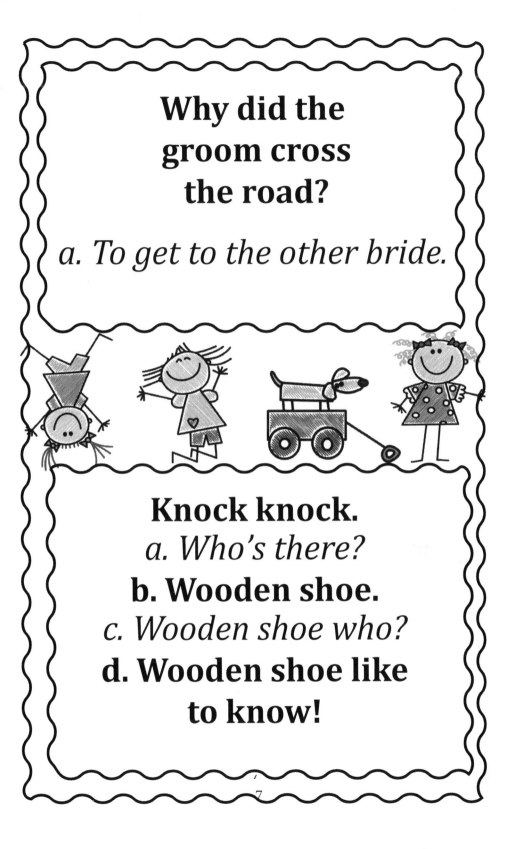

Knock knock.
a. Who's there?
b. Wooden shoe.
c. Wooden shoe who?
d. Wooden shoe like to know!

What is a bride and groom's favorite ride?

a. The married-go-round!

What do you call a noodle wearing a disguise?

a. An impasta.

Why did the cow jump over the moon?

a. Because if the duck did they'd have to call it the quackn.

Where do you buy medicine for pigs and chickens?

a. At the farmacy.

Why didn't the duck go into the ocean?

a. Because he was afraid of the quacken!

When should you put grass in the washing machine?

a. When you're doing the lawndry.

Where do matadors eat dinner?

a. At the tay-bull.

What do you give a pig with sunburn?

a. Oinkment.

What do you get when you cross a genie with a shark?

a. Something that

will grant you three fishes.

Father: Son, why does this coffee taste like dirt?

a. Kid: You told me you wanted it ground!

Where did Cinderella get a boat?

a. From her ferry godmother.

What do you call a man in debt?

a. Owen.

What did the phones do at their wedding?

a. They exchanged rings.

What did the police do to the woman after she robbed a coffee shop?

a. They took her mugshot.

Where does the book go to hike?

a. To the paper trail.

What do you call a gym that's been destroyed?

a. The wreck center.

Kid: Dad, what's a blind stag called?

a. Dad: No eye-deer.

What do you call a large pickle?

a. A big dill!

Dad: Can you tie your shoes?

a. Son: I can knot.

What do you call a suspicious shark?

a. Fishy.

How do you kill a slug?

a. You a-salt it.

Knock knock.
a. Who's there?
b. Dishes.
c. Dishes who?
d. Dishes the police, let us in at once!

Will you remember me tomorrow?

a. Yes.

b. Will you remember on week from now?

c. Yes.

d. Will you remember me next year?

e. Yes.

f. Knock knock.

g. Who's there?

h. You already forgot me!

When should you give your scarecrow a promotion?

a. When it's out-standing in its field.

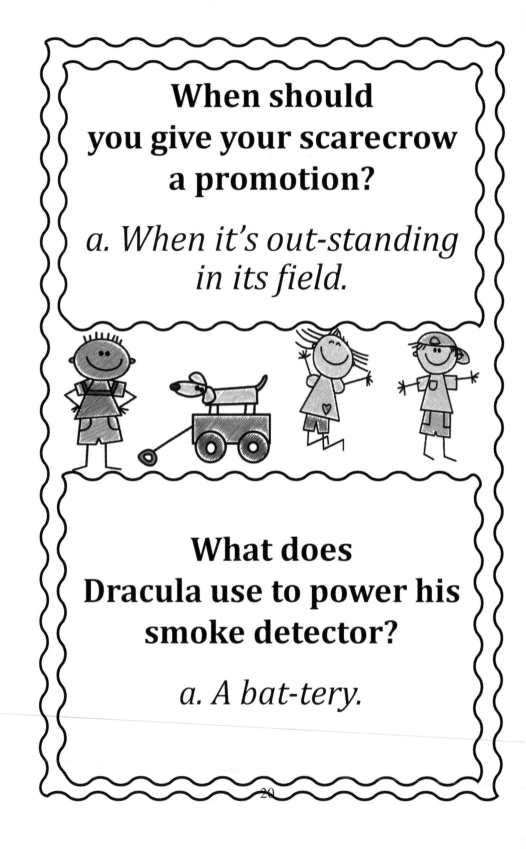

What does Dracula use to power his smoke detector?

a. A bat-tery.

How do you teach a conductor?

a. You train him.

What do you call an author with no left arm?

a. A righter.

Daughter: Should we take the rake with us?

a. No, leaf it at home.

Where does a lumberjack go when he needs new clothes?

a. To the chopping mall.

What should you eat at the beach?

a. A sand-wich.

Who did the ghost fall in love with?

a. His ghoulfriend.

What did the mother say when she saw her son kissing his piggy bank?

a. "Put your money where your mouth is."

Where do astronauts go to drink?

a. To the space bar.

What's the best way to watch steps?

a. Stair at them.

How do you drown a kitchen?

a. Sink it.

When is the best time to buy a boat?

a. When there's a sail.

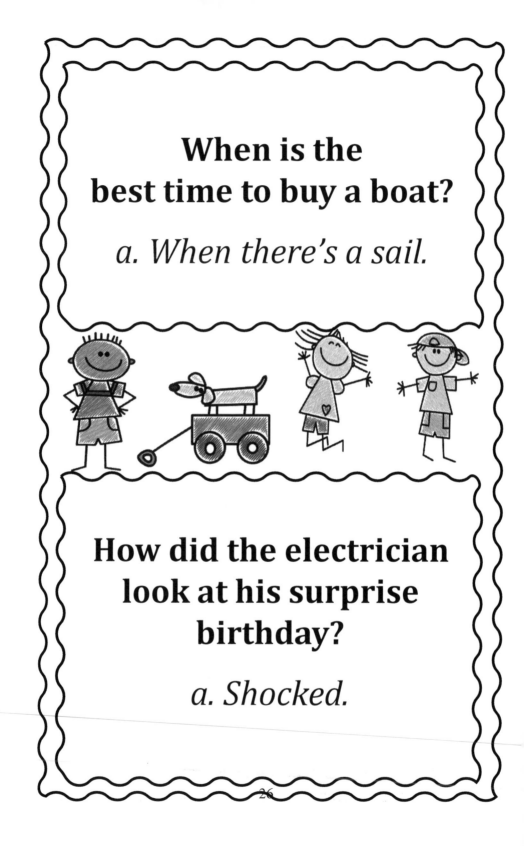

How did the electrician look at his surprise birthday?

a. Shocked.

How do you kill hair?

a. Die it.

What award do you give someone with great door-knocking skills?

a. A no-bell prize.

How do you tell your dog you love her from far away?

a. You collar.

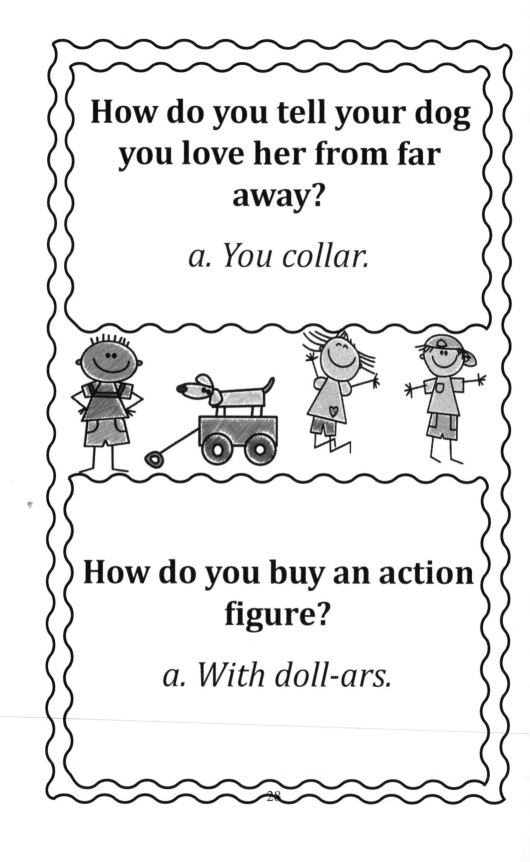

How do you buy an action figure?

a. With doll-ars.

What do you call a dumb lollipop?

a. A sucker.

A mother is trying to get her daughter to eat her carrots, so she tells her, "They're good for your eyes.

a. Her daughter puts her carrots in front of her eyes and says, "That's not true, I can't see a thing!"

Why did the dog sit in the shade?

a. Because he didn't want to be a hot dog.

Father: How many belts do you earn in martial arts?

a. Daughter: A kung-few.

Why did the orange roll only halfway up the hill?

a. Because it ran out of juice.

What do you call a garbage bin that doesn't work?

a. A trash can't.

What has hands but no arms?

a. A clock.

What is the best country for celebrating Thanksgiving?

a. Turkey.

What superhero should you call when you have wrinkly clothes?

a. Iron Man.

Why was the semi-painted wall so cold?

a. Because it only had one coat.

What do you call an unmarried woman that you haven't seen in a long time?

a. Miss.

What do you call a snake building a house?

a. A boa constructor.

What state has the best writers?

a. Pencil-vania.

What did the digital clock say to its mom?

a. Look Ma, no hands!

What do zombies use when they play monopoly?

a. A die.

Why was Winnie the Pooh so chilly?

a. Because he was a little bare.

What do you call a British man who uses the restroom a lot?

a. Lou.

What do you get when you cross a snail and a porcupine?

a. A slow poke.

What do you call a witch that makes honey?

a. A spelling bee.

Do you think that cat would be a good animal to name a tree after?

a. No, but a dogwood.

Where do you go to invest in soup?

a. The stock market.

What do you call a man who's good with money?

a. Bill.

What did the baker do at the touching wedding?

a. He tiered up.

How do you make a handkerchief dance?

a. Put a little boogie in it.

What kind of dancing should you do at a playground?

a. Swing.

What does a snowman eat for breakfast?

a. Snowflakes.

What do you call an adorable angle?

a. Acute.

What is the most delicious number?

a. Pi.

What do you call a man who is good at painting?

a. Art.

Did the painter have a hard time moving in?

a. No, he moved everything easily.

How do you keep track of tree trunks?

a. Keep a log.

How do you find a website for chains?

a. Just click the link.

What is the most annoying kind of sauce?

a. Pest-o.

How do you annoy a dog?

a. Tick him off.

What is the best way to watch videos of water?

a. Stream them.

How do chickens get discounts?

a. They use coop-ons.

What did the volcano say to his sweetheart?

a. I lava you.

What has a face but no eyes?

a. A clock.

How do you keep your pockets from being stolen?

a. Start a pocket watch.

What is the most delicious hairstyle?

a. A bun.

Why did the man get his potato a perm?

a. Because he wanted curly fries.

What did the fast tomato say to the slow tomato?

a. Ketchup.

What did the hotdog do when it was scared?

a. It mustard up

the courage.

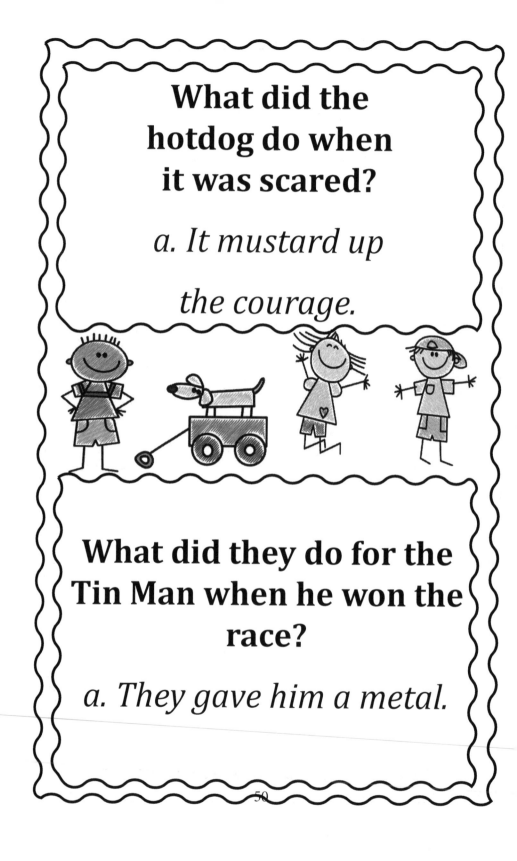

What did they do for the Tin Man when he won the race?

a. They gave him a metal.

What do you get when you have a 20-ton duck?

a. An earthquack.

What do you get when you cross a parakeet with an automobile?

a. A flying car-pet.

Made in the USA
Monee, IL
11 December 2019